EAGLE DREAMS

Written by
Sheryl McFarlane
Illustrated by
Ron Lightburn

PHILOMEL BOOKS

A damp chill lingered in the autumn air the day the veterinarian rattled up the driveway lined with ~~trees~~. leafless poplars. The farmer's son had found a bald eagle with a broken wing.

The farmer was waiting when the vet's truck pulled in. "Robin's got this foolish notion that we can keep the thing," the farmer muttered as he led the vet past fields that grew mud instead of winter rye. They climbed the hill where the forest met the farm. "The boy's a dreamer. Who has time for injured birds? This year I barely got my hay in."

That morning, before he'd found the eagle, Robin had leapt and twirled beneath the shadow of the fir so tall its bleached crown glinted silver in the sun. He'd spread his arms like the wings of eagles soaring overhead. And if someone had asked, he would have told them that he flew, at least inside his head.

Now as Robin waited, he shivered despite the warmth of the afternoon sun. "You'll fly again. I promise," he whispered to the injured bird.

"I kept the crows away," Robin proudly told the vet, when she reached the fir.

The eagle's wing was torn, a bone had snapped and its breathing came in ragged gasps. "It may not survive the shock," the vet explained.

The farmer shook his head. "Best to end its suffering." But Robin answered with a look as wild as the injured eagle's.

The weakened bird barely struggled when they wrapped it in a blanket. The vet reached into her bag. "Right now I'd say don't get your hopes too high."

The vet showed Robin how to splint the wing, explaining that its bones were far too fragile for plaster casts. As she worked, she talked about how eagles sometimes hit power lines when hunting for their prey.

"It's like tripping when you run to catch a ball. You're too busy looking up to check your feet." The vet glanced from the farmer to his son. "The wing is set, but the job is far from done. Now it will need constant care and feeding until its wing heals and those damaged feathers are replaced."

Robin's eyes glowed with willingness, but his father's eyes said no.

"I'll do my chores. I promise," Robin pleaded.

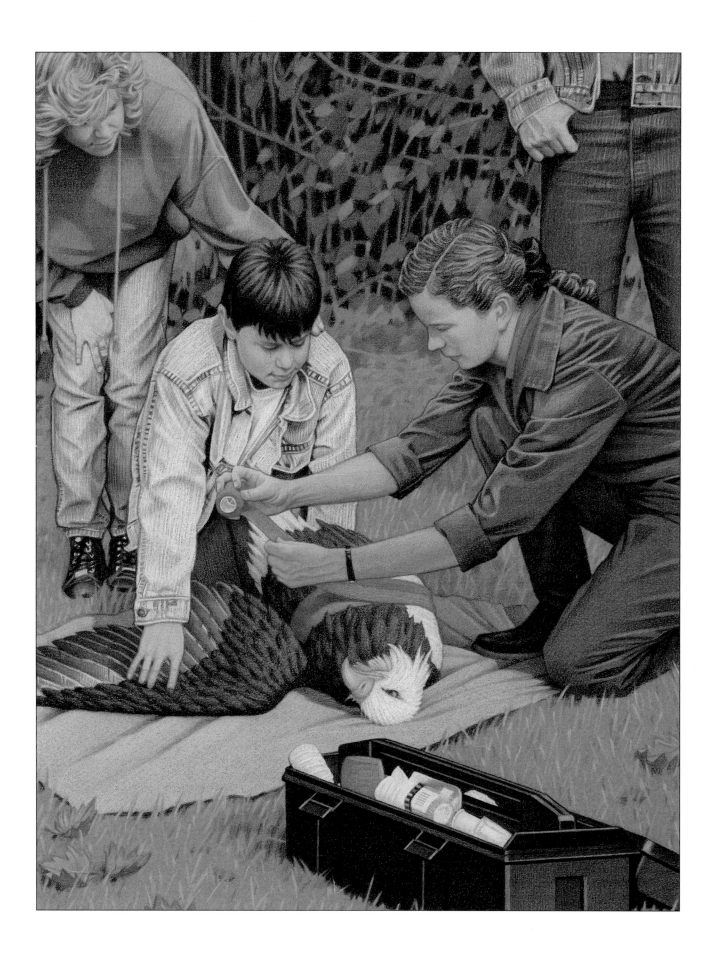

But the farmer remembered too many times when he had seen his son in the forest beyond the biggest barn, slipping on the mossy logs and rocks, while the garden went unweeded. Or running through the fields of golden corn and hay, while other boys his age helped with the threshing. Or swinging from a rope high above the ground, while the chickens went unfed.

Then a shudder shook the giant bird to life and Robin cast a hopeful glance toward his mother.

"All right," the farmer sighed. "But you heard the vet, Son. Don't get your hopes too high."

Robin whooped and danced a rubber-booted jig before calming down to listen to the vet go through a list of things to do each day.

"One last thing," the vet warned. "That eagle's wild. It'll never make a pet."

A few days later, Robin and his mother drove out to see the ranger in the park. Eagles, gulls and crows lined the trees, waiting for a chance to pluck a tasty treat from the shallow waters of the spawning creek. Mother and son filled the truck with enough salmon to feed the injured bird all winter.

The eagle's home became a weathered cedar shed that kept out winter storms. The vet came by often to check up on the bird and on the boy.

By the end of winter holidays, the eagle's wing had healed enough to take the bandages off. The vet helped Robin move the bird to an unused bullpen shaded by the barn. Now there would be room to exercise its weakened wing.

At first his father grumbled about neglected chores, but Robin kept his promise. Sometimes he longed to climb to the swallows' nest above the hayloft or stalk the barnyard cat dozing in the sun. But when the cows stamped and swished their tails and mooed impatiently, Robin hurried over. And like his mother working down the line of cows, he'd soothe them with a gentle word or pat before milking. But his thoughts hovered over the eagle in his care.

There were no complaints about the eagle now, except from the barnyard geese who kept their distance from the bullpen.

Robin hauled a massive tree stump into the bullpen with the tractor. When the eagle's wing grew stronger, he watched the daily progress of its glide. Each day it gobbled up the fish and looked for more. It was hard work to satisfy an eagle's endless appetite.

One crisp morning when the smell of apple blossoms filled the air, Robin heard the bird's high-pitched squeal. An eagle circling overhead returned the call. It swooped down suddenly and Robin reached the pen in time to see a fish fall from the eagle's talons.

"Its mate," Robin's mother smiled. "It will stay nearby."

The eagle perched atop the stump like royalty.

Spreading massive wings, it glided to the ground. It would soon need a larger pen to build strength for the long flights essential for survival in the wild.

When the farmer volunteered the empty barn, Robin stared at his father in surprise. The farmer flashed a sheepish grin and mumbled something about a tractor that needed fixing.

The next time the vet drove the driveway lined with leafy green, her truck kicked up a cloud of summer dust.

Robin led the way in silence, knowing that the eagle's time had come. But a smile touched the corners of his mouth when he peeked into the barn through a crack in the door. The eagle's crown of white shone majestic in the dusty light. And with its wings poised for flight, the eagle called out its anger at the constraints the barn imposed, not caring why but only when it was that it could go. *eagerness to go.*

Robin swung the doors wide open and all of them — the vet, the boy, his father and his mother — watched the eagle swoop through the doors with a scream so full of wildness they could only stand in silence.

Later in the day, Robin and his father climbed the hill that overlooked their farm. They sat beneath the shadow of the fir so tall its bleached crown glinted silver in the sun. And watched the eagle soar above their heads so high, calling to its mate.

"Will it be all right?" Robin asked.

The farmer hesitated before he reached out to his son and drew him near. "I hope so, Son," he said.

Robin sits at his bedroom window when the summer sun has given way to twilight stars. He sees the giant fir atop the hill where bald eagles often perch. He watches for their silhouettes against the sky when he should be asleep.

And in his dreams Robin flies with them above his father's fields of golden corn and hay and over cool green forests to the shoreline with its misty fogs that taste of salt and fish and seaweed.

To a world where bald eagles flourish
along with the dreams they continue to inspire.
S.M.

In memory of my father.
Thanks to Janice, Steve, Kevin, Tracy
and the Royal British Columbia Museum.
R.L.

Text copyright © 1994 by Sheryl McFarlane
Illustrations copyright © 1994 by Ron Lightburn
All rights reserved. This book, or parts thereof, may not be reproduced
in any form without permission in writing from the publisher.
First American Edition published in 1995 by Philomel Books, a division of
The Putnam & Grosset Group, 200 Madison Avenue, New York, NY 10016.
Originally published in 1994 by Orca Book Publishers, Victoria.
Philomel Books, Reg. U.S. Pat. & Tm. Off. Printed in Hong Kong.
Book design by Ron Lightburn.

Library of Congress Cataloging-in-Publication Data
McFarlane, Sheryl. Eagle dreams / Sheryl McFarlane;
illustrated by Ron Lightburn.   p.   cm.
Summary: Robin finds a wounded bald eagle and, with the help of
a veterinarian, nurses her back to health. [1. Bald eagle—Fiction.
2. Eagles—Fiction 3. Wildlife rescue—Fiction.]
I. Lightburn, Ron, ill. II. Title. PZ7.M1665Eag
1994   [E]—dc20   93-21232 CIP AC
ISBN 0-399-22695-8
1 3 5 7 9 10 8 6 4 2
First Impression

Masters of Music

THE WORLD'S GREATEST COMPOSERS

The Life and Times of

Franz Peter Schubert

Mitchell Lane
PUBLISHERS

P.O. Box 619
Bear, Delaware 19701

Masters of Music
THE WORLD'S GREATEST COMPOSERS

Titles in the Series

The Life and Times of...

Visit us on the web: www.mitchelllane.com
Comments? email us: mitchelllane@mitchelllane.com

Masters of Music
THE WORLD'S GREATEST COMPOSERS

The Life and Times of
Franz Peter Schubert

by John Bankston

Copyright © 2004 by Mitchell Lane Publishers, Inc. All rights reserved. No part of this book may be reproduced without written permission from the publisher. Printed and bound in the United States of America.

Printing 1   2   3   4   5   6   7   8   9

Library of Congress Cataloging-in-Publication Data
Bankston, John, 1974-
    The life and times of Franz Peter Schubert / John Bankston.
        p. cm. — (Masters of music. World's greatest composers)
Summary: A biography of the nineteenth-century Austrian composer.
Includes bibliographical references (p.   ) and index.
    ISBN 1-58415-177-3 (library bound)
    1. Schubert, Franz, 1797-1828—Juvenile literature. 2. Composers—Austria—Biography—
Juvenile literature. [1. Schubert, Franz, 1797-1828. 2. Composers.] I. Title. II. Series.
    ML3930.S38 B25 2003
    780'.92--dc21

                                                                                    2002011056

ABOUT THE AUTHOR: Born in Boston, Massachusetts, John Bankston has written over three dozen biographies for young adults profiling scientists like Jonas Salk and Alexander Fleming, celebrities like Mandy Moore and Alicia Keys, great achievers like Alfred Nobel, and master musicians like Mozart. An avid reader and writer, he has had a lifelong love of music history. He has worked in Los Angeles, California as a producer, screenwriter and actor. Currently he is in pre-production on *Dancing at the Edge*, a semi-autobiographical film he hopes to film in Portland, Oregon. Last year he completed his first young adult novel, *18 to Look Younger.*

PUBLISHER'S NOTE: This story is based on the author's extensive research, which he believes to be accurate. Documentation of such research is contained on page 46.

The internet sites referenced herein were all active as of the publication date. Due to the fleeting nature of some Web sites, we cannot guarantee they will all be active when you are reading this book.

Contents

The Life and Times of
Franz Peter Schubert

by John Bankston

* For Your Information

Perhaps the most successful composer of his generation, Ludwig van Beethoven enjoyed a level of fame and fortune Franz Schubert could only dream of. Schubert idolized Beethoven so much, he once sold his textbooks to buy a ticket to one of his operas.

Idolizing Beethoven

Ludwig van Beethoven was dying. He was suffering from kidney and liver disease, perhaps made worse by alcohol. By February of 1827, he knew his life would soon be over. Beethoven was famous in a way no composer before him had been—not Wolfgang Mozart, not Joseph "Papa" Haydn.

While many of Beethoven's fellow citizens in Vienna were aware of his illness, one man—a virtually unknown young composer—was especially distressed by the great man's struggles.

The composer was Franz Schubert, an early part of the Romantic Movement in music. Beethoven was Schubert's idol. As a teenager, Franz loved his work so much that he sold some of his school books to pay for a ticket to a performance of Beethoven's opera *Fidelio*. Later, he dedicated a set of piano variations to Beethoven with the words "by his admirer and worshipper, Franz Schubert." And his Ninth Symphony contains part of the "Ode to Joy" theme that Beethoven used in his own Ninth ("Choral") Symphony.

Franz Schubert drew inspiration from the great composers who came before him, like Beethoven, Wolfgang Mozart and Joseph Haydn. Yet during his brief lifetime, he not only carved out his own style, but later became the composer most identified with the Romantic movement in music.

"His ideal was Beethoven," school friend Benedikt Randhartinger once recalled. "All other composers mattered little to him."

According to one story, Beethoven took the time to read some of Schubert's work as he lay on his deathbed. Reading through those compositions, Beethoven exclaimed, "Truly, in Schubert there is a divine spark!" He saw in the man's work a genius few had recognized.

But no one is sure if the two men actually met face to face. Although they only lived a few miles from each other, their lives were worlds apart. Beethoven was celebrated, Schubert obscure, a 30-year-old who'd spent his life struggling against poverty, depression and a disease which was slowly killing him. Unable to support a wife and family, he'd never married. And until recently, music publishers had rejected his work.

A friend of both Schubert and Beethoven, Anselm Hüttenbrenner, was by Beethoven's bedside on the evening of March 26. Suddenly a flash of lightning illuminated the room. The composer raised his arm, his fist tightly clenched. Then he fell back onto his bed.

Ludwig van Beethoven was dead.

Three days later, 20,000 mourners attended the funeral. Schubert was one of 36 torchbearers who walked alongside the coffin as it was carried to the gravesite, an enormous honor for the young man.

A poet named Franz Grillparzer, a friend of Schubert's, delivered the funeral oration. "He was an artist," Grillparzer said, referring to Beethoven. "Who shall stand beside him?"

Afterwards Schubert hung out with friends until the night's wee hours, talking about Beethoven. Although he mourned the loss of his idol, it's possible that Schubert believed that Grillparzer's words were directed at him. All he needed was a bit more luck, some dedication and his work could be as admired as Beethoven's.

But there would be no luck.

In less than two years, Franz Peter Schubert died. Though he was buried just a few yards from his idol Beethoven, it seemed that his reputation went into the ground with him. Even one of his friends, referring to two of Vienna's most famous composers, wrote that "In spite of all the admiration I have felt for my dear friend, we shall never make a Mozart or a Haydn out of him."

The friend was wrong. After his death, Schubert's works were discovered. It took several decades, but Schubert's reputation has grown immensely despite his lack of success in life. Today he is regarded as one of our great composers. ◆

THE ROMANTICS

"When I wished to sing of love, it turned to sorrow. And when I wished to sing of sorrow, it was transformed for me into love," Franz Schubert complained as he described the kind of energy that made his songs unique. His style of composition made him a leader among the Romantics, although his contributions were not fully appreciated until after his death.

The Romantics were artists who embraced strong emotion, imagination and rebellion against society. In his brief lifetime, Franz would know pain, loss and heartbreak—just as nearly every human being does eventually. What set him apart was his ability to turn these experiences into compositions, everything from famous works like "Death and the Maiden" and "Ave Maria" to simple jottings as a teen. Franz Schubert made his life into art.

The Romantics were artistic rebels. Like 60s-era rock stars describing the flaws of the older generation and hip-hop artists rapping about society's prejudices, the Romantics were critical of those in power and embraced change, while looking to the power of love and nature.

Before the romantic period there was the Enlightenment, a time where the rational was championed. It was the age of reason, which celebrated the mind. Romantics celebrated the heart.

The artists of the period found their inspirations in the uncontrolled freedoms of nature. From writers like the young novelist Mary Shelley (whose book *Frankenstein* was published when she was 21) and poet Lord Byron to the dark and gothic paintings of John Henry Fuseli, the artists of the period challenged social conventions and later the world they lived in. Even the living arrangements of the older generation were avoided. Many Romantics lived together without benefit of marriage or in small groups similar to the hippie communes of the late 1960s.

Musically, Ludwig van Beethoven was a bridge between the Classical and Romantic Periods. Although he belonged to the older (and criticized) generation, his influence on composers like Franz Schubert was unmistakable. Just as Franz picked up aspects of Beethoven's style, in his middle age the older composer experimented with romantic forms. His piano sonata in E minor instructed the performer to use "feeling and expression throughout" while his Pastoral Symphony utilized natural and "romantic" images such as a violent storm and the lush countryside.

Even more than Beethoven, Franz Schubert's music was deeply rooted in nature's poetry, the pain of lost love and sympathy for society's powerless. He was a true Romantic.

Franz Peter Schubert was born in 1797 in the northwestern section of Vienna. The unit his family lived in consisted of a kitchen and one large room, a typical situation in Vienna at that time.

CHAPTER 2

A Positive Note

In 1797, life in Austria began to change as Napoleon Bonaparte gave early evidence that he was a small man with big dreams. In his first major campaign at the head of a French army, he defeated Austrian armies in several battles in Northern Italy. He made preparations to cross the Alps and invade Austria itself. The Austrians quickly concluded a peace treaty.

While death arrived on the battlefield for thousands of Austrians, one life arrived in the northwestern section of Vienna to the Schubert family. Franz Theodor Schubert was the principal of a small primary school in the city's suburb of Himmelpfortgrund. His wife Elisabeth was a locksmith's daughter. The couple already had three boys: Ignaz, Ferdinand and Karl. Their apartment—just a primitive kitchen and one large room—was in a building with 15 other units. Such crowding was typical of Vienna at the time. More than 3,000 people were jammed into just 86 houses in Himmelpfortgrund. But the family's meager circumstances didn't prevent them from celebrating the birth of a son on January 31. They named him Franz Peter.

In the 1900s, Adolf Hitler's ambitions would devastate Europe and threaten the world. Over one hundred years before, Napoleon Bonaparte (shown here) had similar dreams of conquest. Before his famous defeat at Waterloo, hundreds of thousands of lives would be sacrificed to his ambition.

Because of his hard work and the success of his school, Franz Theodor purchased a larger house four years later. It meant more room for the family, which was increased later that year with the birth of a daughter, Maria Theresia. She would be the fifth and final child to survive past infancy or early childhood of a total of 14 born to Franz Theodor and Elisabeth. This grim statistic was normal for the time, but no less tragic. Kids who survived were seen as miracles.

During Franz's childhood, war raged not far from his front door. In 1805, the French army mounted an invasion of Austria and won a decisive victory at the Battle of Austerlitz, which claimed nearly 20,000 lives on both sides. As a result, Napoleon installed himself in Schönbrunn, Emperor Francis's magnificent palace in the heart of Vienna. He also forced the Austrians to give him some of their territories. When the Austrians revolted four years later, they were swiftly defeated. So as Franz grew up, French soldiers on Vienna streets were a common sight.

But no matter what was happening outside, music provided a pleasant diversion inside the Schuberts' residence. Franz Theodor was a skillful musician. Although he primarily played the cello, he was familiar enough with other stringed instruments to provide lessons to his offspring. For fun, several of the boys would join him as a string quartet with Ignaz and Ferdinand on the violins while Franz Peter played the viola. His older brothers saw playing music as little more than a pleasant distraction, but for young Franz it was something more.

He had a gift. From the moment he began playing an instrument—whether it was the piano, the viola or the violin—or singing, his talents were obvious. He learned quickly. He never had to be asked to practice. And whenever his father played a wrong note, Franz would gently interrupt and point out the error.

Franz Theodor recognized his son's abilities. He also quickly recognized that he had taught the boy all he could. So he arranged for him to take lessons with a professional music teacher, church organist Michael Holzer. While Holzer provided the youngster with an excellent grounding in singing and playing several instruments, he found that he had a challenging task. "Whenever I wished to impart something new to him, he always knew it already," he would later recall. "I didn't need to teach him, only to watch him in silent astonishment."

His brother Ferdinand wrote about the results of this combination of hard work and natural ability: "In his 11th year he (Franz) was a first soprano in the Liechtenal church. Already at that time he delivered everything with the most appropriate expression; in those days he also played a violin solo in the organ-loft of the church and already composed small songs, string quartets and pianoforte pieces."

Franz was fortunate to be growing up in a city where musicians were valued. Youngsters with musical potential were often sent to special schools where their gifts could be nurtured. One of the best was the Stadtkonvikt, the Imperial and Royal Court Seminary. A forbidding place, this boarding school was well known for both the top musical training it provided and its inadequate facilities. Students who were admitted there learned both the intricacies of musicianship and how to cope with hunger. Food and warmth were scarce, but quality musical instruction was abundant.

Franz's opportunity came in 1808. The Imperial and Royal Chapel advertised an opening for two new sopranos in its small choir. Earning the spot would also guarantee admission to the Stadtkonvikt. So Franz spent several months preparing for the audition. It was in front of the Court Music Director, Antonio Salieri, who had been a rival of the famous composer Wolfgang Amadeus Mozart.

Franz was accepted. So in early October, he joined 130 other boys, all wearing the school's distinctive white neckerchief, brown coat and long shorts.

At the school, Franz studied the works of great composers like George Frideric Handel, Mozart and of course Beethoven. The boy was also a talented violinist in the student orchestra, where he formed a lifelong friendship.

A talented composer at an age when most children are in grade school, Wolfgang Mozart (shown here) is one of the best-known child prodigies in history. From a young age, Franz Schubert displayed similar gifts. He was a talented musician as a boy and wrote many of his compositions while still in his teens.

Nine years older than Franz, Josef von Spaun was studying the law and working part-time as a student musical director when the boy joined his fledgling orchestra. "Schubert, who was barely twelve years old, played the second violin in the orchestra," Spaun would later write. "His remarkable feeling for the works being performed made those around him aware of his exceptional talent and soon the little fellow was put at the head of the orchestra, all the adults willingly subordinating themselves to him."

Composer Antonio Salieri's reputation was nearly destroyed over his rivalry with Mozart and unfounded rumors that he'd killed the young composer. In his later life, his reputation was restored by his gifts as an educator. He instructed hundreds of talented young musicians, including Franz Schubert.

The value of Spaun's friendship was both immediate and long-lasting. Spaun supplied the boy with manuscript paper for his compositions and companionship for his loneliness. He wrote that Franz once told him, "You are my favorite in the whole Seminary, I have no other friend here."

For the first several years at the Seminary, Schubert did well in his studies and received an excellent grounding in music. Then several important events happened almost simultaneously in 1812.

His mother, Elisabeth fell ill that spring and died from a fever. Franz may have been describing what happened in a story called "My Dream" that he wrote a decade later: "Then came news of my mother's death. I hastened back to see her; and my father, softened by grief, didn't hinder my return. I saw her lying dead. Tears streamed out of my eyes."

The youngster was already writing music by this time. Salieri was impressed enough to begin giving private lessons to Franz. The Italian composer had been well acquainted with Mozart—perhaps he saw in Franz some of the great composer's talent without the attitude. When Franz ran out of music paper, he used a ruler and pen to make his own. Nothing stopped him.

Then his voice broke as he entered puberty. In a humorous vein, he scribbled "Schubert, Franz, crowed for the last time on 26 July 1812" on a piece of sheet music. That meant the end of his choral scholarship. But he was eligible for other forms of financial assistance—known as endowments—that would allow him to remain at the Seminary. However, he was spending so much time on music that some of his other studies were beginning to suffer. In the next year, he wrote a great deal of music, which included his First Symphony.

Then he appears to have made a decision.

The Emperor himself, Francis I, signed a document that stipulated the conditions under which Franz could remain at the Seminary. It contained the fateful words, "singing and music are but a subsidiary matter, while good morals and diligence in study are of prime importance and an indispensable duty for all those who wish to enjoy the advantages of an Endowment."

But to Franz Schubert, even at the age of 16, music was not a subsidiary matter. It was his life.

He would later write, "I have come into the world for no purpose but to compose."

Spaun described what happened next. Schubert decided "to leave the Seminary and to give up his studies as well, in order to devote his life to art undisturbed," he wrote.

That last word was to prove of vital importance. Art became the most important part of Schubert's life. But it would hardly be undisturbed.

According to Spaun, "He (Franz) told me that secretly he often wrote down his thoughts in music, but his father must not know about it, as he was dead against his devoting himself to music."

His father had good reason for his opposition. The life of a musician was very difficult. The elder Franz was probably not a tyrannical man, forcing his will on his son. He wanted young Franz to be able to make a good living. So he had something else in mind for Franz besides music: joining the family business as an educator.

Franz Schubert saw his entire future—mapped out by his father and racing toward him like a speeding bullet.

FRENCH EXPANSION

Just as Adolf Hitler's ambitions radically affected Europe in the twentieth century, Napoleon Bonaparte's dreams devastated the continent more than 100 years earlier. Born on August 15, 1769 in Ajaccio, Corsica, Napoleon was commissioned as a second lieutenant when he was only 16 and was elected lieutenant colonel of the Corsican Volunteers before his 24th birthday.

He began his rise to power in the aftermath of the French Revolution, which began in 1789. In 1793, revolutionaries executed former King Louis XVI and the new government declared war on England and Spain. The decision was based in part on revolutionary leader George Jacques Danton's principle of "natural frontiers." He believed France was not bounded by the lines created on a map, but only by natural boundaries. To him all the land between the Atlantic Ocean, the Pyrenees, the Rhine and the Alps belonged to France.

Beyond Danton's point of view, the newly composed French government, which was run by the people and not by the royals, threatened other European monarchies. Between Danton's philosophy and the insecurities of countries like England, France faced seemingly never-ending conflict.

The "natural frontiers" policy of French expansion also helped to expand the power of Napoleon. Beginning in 1795 with his leadership of the French army in Italy, Napoleon's war machine raged across Europe. In 1804 Napoleon crowned himself Emperor. By giving himself a title not terribly different from the king who had been overthrown just over a decade before, Napoleon lost some of the popular support he'd won. Still his victories continued as his efforts dissolved the Holy Roman Empire in 1806, which included Austria and dated back to 1232. By 1810, out of a European population numbering 175 million, over 50 million were under the control of France.

Napoleon finally overextended himself when he invaded Russia in 1812 with an army of about 500,000 men. Just as Hitler's expansion during World War II was halted by the brutal Russian winter, Napoleon's forces were devastated by freezing temperatures, warfare and disease. Only about 10,000 troops survived.

Napoleon regrouped, but in 1814 the French Army was defeated by a coalition that included Austria, Prussia and England. Napoleon resigned as Emperor and was exiled to the Mediterranean island of Elba. He escaped early the following year and regained power. But he was finally defeated in the decisive battle of Waterloo in June, 1815. He was exiled again, this time to the tiny South Atlantic island of St. Helena. He died there on May 5, 1821.

Schubert was swept away by 16-year-old Therese Grob. However, she wasn't interested in the poor, struggling composer. Nevertheless, he dedicated many of his early compositions to her.

CHAPTER

3

The Dream

So instead of graduating from the Stadtkonvikt, 16-year-old Franz Schubert spent most of 1814 at Vienna's St. Anna Teacher's Training College. Illustrations from the time reveal a good-looking young man, with thick brown hair, deep-set eyes and pensive brows. Alcohol and heavy Austrian meals would eventually destroy his looks, but at 17 he was mainly struggling with his height. Just five foot one at adulthood, Franz coped with the issues faced by all shorter men, but in nineteenth century Vienna his stature had one advantage. In combination with his poor eyesight, it made him ineligible to be drafted into the army—which at that time was for a period of at least 14 years.

Avoiding army service was the only good news for Franz, who watched as fellow students earned positions as court and church musicians while he was rejected for every job he applied for. His abilities didn't impress anyone enough to hire him, and even a letter of recommendation from Salieri didn't help. As a teenager, Mozart had been a concertmaster for an archbishop. At nearly the same age, Franz found himself moving back home and working for his dad.

Being a teacher wasn't the worst job in the world. It just wasn't what Franz wanted to do. His pay was terrible and he was in charge of teaching children as young as six years old. Some days he probably felt more like a babysitter than an educator. "It is true that they irritated me whenever I tried to create and I lost the idea," he later confessed. Proving how ill-suited he was for the job, he admitted, "Naturally, I would beat them up."

An uninspiring job can be a gift for a creative mind. Had Franz been employed as a court composer or in another musical post with steady pay and respect, he might have been happier. But he wouldn't have had as much creative freedom. His work would have been assigned by a boss; there would be little time for his own creations.

Instead, composing filled Franz Schubert's life. He lived for the end of each tedious day in the classroom, and poured his energy into writing music. His talent was quickly obvious. His first sacred work, the Mass in F Major was performed in Franz's local church in October 1814. Then the larger St. Augustine Church presented it as well.

The mass did more than give Franz his first taste of success. It also gave the 17-year-old teenager his first taste of love.

Therese Grob was a 16-year-old soprano whose solo singing in both productions was a highlight for Franz. He was mesmerized. Although he described her to friends as "not particularly pretty," his seeming disinterest was a facade, an act. His real feelings became apparent once he started composing songs inspired by Therese. This is an artist's best way of expressing their true feelings, but the young soprano was immune to Franz's overtures.

The aspiring composer was poor, with few professional job prospects. All the songs in the world weren't going to change that. Nineteenth century composers had fewer ways to earn a living than musicians do today, and Schubert had failed at all of them. He'd been unable to land a job in music, he didn't have rich patrons paying him to write and publishers weren't interested. Franz Schubert was an amateur and a dreamer. Therese wasn't interested. A few years later she married a baker.

Franz was heartbroken by her rejection. He never forgot her.

Between 1813 and 1816, Franz composed 400 different works, including many that were based on the poems of Johann Wolfgang von Goethe. One was "Margaret at the Spinning Wheel," taken from a scene in Goethe's play *Faust* and dedicated to Therese. Another was the *Erlkönig*, which many people regard as Schubert's first masterpiece. His friend Spaun sent a packet of Schubert's work to Goethe in 1816. But the famous author sent back the packet without making any comments.

Then a few years later Franz himself would write to Goethe, "Should I succeed with the dedication of these settings of your poems in expressing my boundless admiration of Your Excellency, and at the same time in earning perhaps something of respect for my unworthy self, the gratification of this wish would be for me the happiest event of my life." Unfortunately, Schubert never got a response on this occasion either.

His early output also included a cantata—his first composition written on commission—and four more symphonies, bringing his total to five before the age of 20. Not even his idol Beethoven had accomplished that.

But despite his musical productivity, Franz was unhappy at home. His father had remarried and his new wife Anna had added several stepbrothers and stepsisters to the family. Even though Franz seems to have gotten along well with his stepmother, who was just 14 years older than he was, it was still hard to concentrate with so many people under the same roof. He was convinced he'd be more successful elsewhere. So he finally made the decision many young people make—to abandon the security of home for the unpredictable land of dreams.

He quit his job. He might have been only a poor schoolteacher—a profession that didn't enjoy much social status—but Franz Schubert had some interesting friends.

He spent many evening hours with Spaun, who continued to push Franz to pursue his dreams and introduced him to Johann Mayrhofer, a law student and poet who asked Schubert to set his words to music. And there was Franz von Schober. Well-bred and well-spoken, Schober got the composer into the best parties and the worst bars. Schubert moved in with Schober, and the two Franzes embarked on a lifestyle at odds with the composer's dreams. Still, it provided temporary escape from the broken heart Schubert was still mending and his own unrealized ambitions.

Like a number of young adults, Franz spent many nights partying. His friends were law students, with solid futures and family money, but Franz had nothing to fall back on. He needed to make his own way in the world. The only way he could do that was to write.

In 1817, he composed over five dozen songs, including one of his more famous works, "Death and the Maiden," and set one of Schober's poems to music. That year, Schober also introduced him to Johann Vogl, a famous baritone singer with the German Opera in Vienna. Schubert would write many of his songs specifically for Vogl. Vogl returned the favor by working to make Schubert better known.

Schubertiads were festive parties featuring lots of food, drink and Franz Schubert performing some of his compositions. Even in his darkest hours, these parties always lifted his spirits.

Franz Schubert's admirable work ethic didn't pay off right away. Publishers weren't interested in buying his songs. Late in 1817, his money ran out. Unwilling to live any longer off his friends' charity, he returned home. In a way, he felt like he was giving up, and the heartbreak he must have felt surely rivaled the one he'd nursed for Therese Grob. Franz needed to be patient.

He'd barely begun working at his father's schoolhouse when he learned that one of his songs, "Lake Erlaff," had been published. It was based on a poem written by Mayrhofer. It brought him a little extra money and, more important, recognition. When some of his music was performed at a local hotel, reviewers praised the young composer's "disciplined yet spontaneous force."

His life began to change. The summer of 1818 brought a job offer from the Hungarian Count Johann Carl Esterházy, who required a music teacher to give lessons to his two teen-aged daughters. The job not only gave Franz a steady wage, it left him plenty of time to compose. It was also the first time he had traveled outside Vienna. "I'm really living at last," he excitedly wrote a friend. His joy was tempered by the way he was treated. Franz Schubert was a member of the count's household staff, forced to live and eat among the servants. His pride was hurt, but not enough to keep him from reportedly having an affair with one of the maids.

Over the next few years, Franz's success as a songwriter increased. One highlight was Vogl's performance of *Erlkönig*. In the beginning, it was his friends who sent his songs to music publishers but as they became widely published, his confidence grew. Although the composer's lack of business instincts kept him from making as much money as he could have, he was able to make a modest living from his songwriting.

As Schubert entered his 20s, he was living his dreams, earning money writing music. Socially he was the center of attention. His friends threw elaborate parties that quickly became known as "Schubertiads." Schubert playing his latest music on the piano was the highlight of evenings that also included games of charades, poetry readings and lots of talk about the hot topics of the day.

Yet while Schubert's music was giving him a great life, his partying was about to take all of that away. ◆

GOETHE

Faustian bargains happen when someone gets what he or she wants but has to trade something even more valuable to receive it. In German folklore, Faust was a magician who bargained with the devil, trading his soul for power.

Franz Schubert didn't make a Faustian bargain when he contacted Johann Wolfgang von Goethe, the author whose dramatic poem was based on the German myth. But Franz probably would have been willing to trade his soul for a taste of success. Such recognition wasn't coming his way. Goethe didn't even send Franz a polite rejection letter. But then again, he was pretty busy, probably too busy to correspond with a teenage wannabe.

Goethe, who was born in 1749, exerted a powerful influence on the cultural and literary life of Europe in the eighteenth century. A German scientist and writer, he gained his greatest fame from lyrical poems and the dramatic epic poem *Faust*, which appeared in two parts. The first part was published in 1808 and the second 24 years later. Perhaps more than any other writer of the time, Goethe's work signaled a break from the mental emphasis of the Enlightenment period and a progression towards the emotions of the Romantics. His work was also part of the "Sturm und Drang," or Storm and Stress literary genre.

Fame arrived for Goethe with the performance of his play *Goetz of Berlichingen* in 1773 when he was in his early 20s. From 1811-1822 he published his autobiography. Goethe was hardly modest—it covered six volumes. "For a man to achieve all that is demanded of him," Goethe once wrote, "he must regard himself as greater than he is."

Goethe did more than write creative poetry and long-winded memoirs. More than 200 years ago, the Industrial Revolution changed Europe when the continent's economy moved from one based on farming to one based on manufacturing. Most saw this as positive progress, but Goethe noted its negative consequences. Today authors write about how computers have altered human relations, but Goethe was the first to point out how relying on machines could be dehumanizing. He believed machines lacked the "human touch" and laboring on them would quickly become routine and soulless.

Beyond social commentary, he was also a scientist. He was again ahead of his time, as he wrote about morphology, a branch of science which looks at the structure of living organisms. His ideas would be used as a cornerstone for Charles Darwin's theories of evolution decades later.

This portrait, completed just three years before the composer's death, shows Franz Schubert's efforts to appear carefree despite the burdens of poverty, heartbreak and a disease that was slowly killing him.

CHAPTER 4

Some Bad Choices

F ranz Schubert had big dreams, ambitions that encompassed everything from opera and symphonies to sonatas and popular songs. What he didn't have was money. For a single man in the eighteenth century, having a steady income was even more important than it is today. Good families with marriageable daughters wouldn't even consider a prospective husband unless he earned a good living.

Most of the time Franz could barely take care of himself, let alone a wife and family. This didn't mean he didn't get lonely. In Vienna, companionship could be purchased. So the composer became a frequenter of prostitutes. But he would pay an enormous price for a few moments of pleasure.

Safe sex was unheard of in the early 1800s but sexually transmitted diseases were not. Just as unprotected sex led to the outbreak of AIDS in the twentieth century, 200 years before it was responsible for the spread of syphilis. It was deadly, it was incurable and early in 1823, Franz Schubert learned he had it.

Franz was admitted to Vienna's General Hospital in May. Throughout the rest of the summer, he struggled against the disease's early symptoms. The illness affected more than just his body. Depression became his constant companion. He'd been working on his Eighth Symphony when he contracted the illness, but it would remain forever uncompleted. Consisting of the two movements that he had finished, it is known today as the "Unfinished Symphony" and is among his most widely performed works. While Schubert didn't intend it that way, one of the themes in the first movement can be sung to the words "This is/the symphony/that Schubert wrote but never finished."

Although he ceased work on the Eighth Symphony, he didn't stop composing. He completed "The Wanderer," a piano fantasy that is one of his best-known projects and *The Fair Maid of the Mill*, the first of his great song cycles.

His creative efforts came as a rash covered his body. He shaved what was left of his hair, replacing it with a wig. He struggled with alcohol. The doctors told him to stop drinking for health reasons. Franz didn't think their orders were very important—he knew he was dying.

Months later, Franz would write a letter that reflected his feelings at the time to one of his friends, Leopold Kupelwieser. "I feel myself to be the unhappiest, most miserable being in the world," he said. "Imagine a man whose health will never be right again, and who in despair makes things worse and worse instead of better. Imagine a man whose brightest hopes have been shattered, to whom the happiness of love and friendship offers at best pain, whose enthusiasm (at least the stimulating kind) for beauty threatens to vanish; and ask yourself, 'Is this not an unhappy, miserable man?'"

In the fall, his syphilis went into remission. That meant that he was better, but not cured. But it was enough to motivate him into another period of productivity.

By now, many of his old friends had married or moved away, but he made new acquaintances—young law students and aspiring musicians. He returned in the summer of 1824 to the Esterházy estate. His former 13-year-old pupil Karoline was now 19 and a beautiful young woman. Several of Schubert's friends believed that he fell in love with her. Given the difference in their social positions and the disease which was continuing to ravage him, nothing could come of it. But he composed piano duets for them to play together. And this time he got to stay in the castle itself rather than in the servants' quarters.

He returned to Vienna in autumn, and his old friends noted a new Franz, a man bursting with vitality and happiness. Perhaps love had cured his blues.

Professionally his life was finally being transformed. Publishers required simple songs they could sell to amateur musicians. Franz became very adept at turning out these works. Although he was still selling his pieces for less than he should have, he was starting to earn a living.

A decade before he'd sold his schoolbooks for a chance to see Beethoven's *Fidelio*. By 1825 *Fidelio*'s star soprano, Anna Milder, was singing Franz's songs. Across the region, other top singers were performing Schubert's music as well. Ecstatic from new success, Franz sent a second packet of his music to Goethe— again there was no response.

When Franz spent several months traveling with Vogl to Upper Austria during the late spring and summer of 1825, he learned he was somewhat better known away from Vienna. From royals to monks, Franz met numerous people who loved his songs and were thrilled to meet their author. The journey also included a visit to Salzburg, the birthplace of Wolfgang Mozart. Franz found a town devastated by Napoleon's war machine and an 1818 fire.

"The town itself made a rather gloomy impression upon me, for the bad weather caused the ancient buildings to look more somber still," he wrote to his brother Ferdinand that September. By this time his best friend Spaun had spent a few summer days with Mozart's son, Franz Xaver, and told him of Schubert's efforts to find success. Franz Xaver could probably relate to the story, for his father had known enormous struggle as well.

In October, Franz returned to Vienna where he was pleased to read good reviews for his music even as publishers continued to pay him. Still, he was struggling and once again aspired to a steady paycheck.

"His name is well known, not only in Vienna, but throughout Germany as a composer of songs and instrumental music," Franz wrote in support of his application to be deputy music director at the Vienna Court in spring of 1826. Describing himself in the letter he went on, "he is at present time without employment, and hopes in the security of a permanent position to be able to realize at last those musical aspirations which he has ever kept before him."

But those aspirations went unfulfilled. He didn't get the job.

So Franz continued doing what he had always done: composing in bed during the morning, hanging out at coffee shops during the day and bars at night. He was overeating and drinking too much. His friends started calling him "Tubby."

For Franz Schubert the party was almost over. ◆

REVOLUTIONS

Franz Schubert's depression and his illness may have obscured, for him, the exciting times in which he lived. For Franz lived his life in the midst of revolution. Political revolutions in France and the Netherlands inspired common people across the continent to demand more freedoms. In the cities, the Industrial Revolution created new jobs and changed the way many people earned their wages. And there were other revolutions. While not all of them were as dramatic, they had a permanent effect on the culture.

Changes arrived in both big ways and small. In the 1700s, men's clothing had been dominated by wigs and powder, showy coats and ruffled shirts. In the 1800s, a style revolution begun by George "Beau" Brummell emphasized the way clothes were tailored, rather than their showiness. Coats and trousers became tighter, accentuating the physique of the man wearing them. For example, in the early nineteenth century, pants made for men were designed to emphasize their calves! Although his influence produced such long-forgotten items as the walking stick and trouser straps, Brummell also created black and white formal wear which led to today's prom attire. He also believed a well-groomed gentleman should bathe, shave and change clothes every day. Before his influence most upper-class men—and women as well—rarely bathed. They relied on heavy perfume to mask their body odors.

Fashion was hardly the only revolution that survived the period. Social revolutions in France produced the country's first divorce law. Prior to 1792, marriage was for life in accordance with the teachings of the Church. However, once the divorce law was enacted it was relatively easy for married couples to split up.

Women had long been seen as second-class citizens and granted few rights. In the early 1800s they began demanding the same freedoms men had won. Although many of their efforts failed, they set the stage for the reforms that occurred in the nineteenth and twentieth centuries. "I do not wish them (women) to have power over men, but over themselves," Mary Wollstonecraft said, discussing her groundbreaking work *Vindication of the Rights of Women*. Published in 1792, it is widely considered to be the first great feminist document.

Power over their own lives was an idea Franz Schubert embraced and one that has survived the test of time.

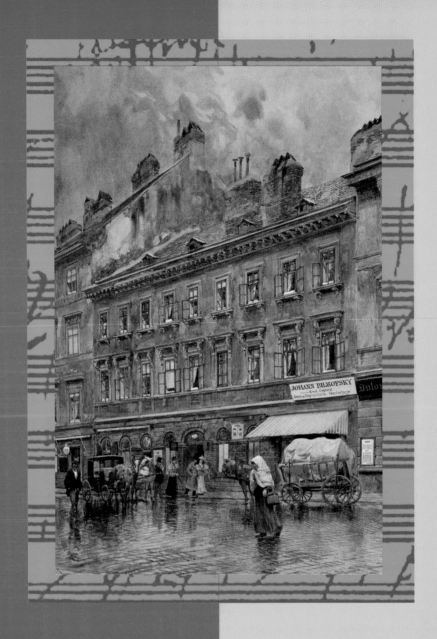

In September 1828, Franz Schubert was so weakened by syphilis that he was unable to care for himself and was forced to move into his brother's home, shown here.

CHAPTER 5

This is the End

F ranz Schubert was an imaginative dreamer who could create works of music that were wonderful flights of fancy. But when he needed to, he could be realistic. He had a fatal illness. With every day's conclusion, Franz knew he was closer to death.

With little time left, Franz put all of his energy into his twin loves: composing and socializing. He began the year by setting still more of Goethe's poems to music; the total now stood at well over 70. During the summer of 1826, he wrote songs based on the plays of William Shakespeare along with what would be his final string quartet. In the fall, he returned to his favorite coffeehouses and enjoyed "Schubertiads" at night. One such event was held at Spaun's house and featured Vogl performing more than 30 of the composer's songs. Besides music, the parties featured plenty of liquor, heavy food and even snowball fights!

During the second half of 1826, Franz's finances improved. His fame grew as well when a reviewer from London's *The Harmonicon* wrote about a performance of Franz's music at a Vienna theater, describing "a revived Overture by Schubert, full of striking effects and well worthy of being better known."

While 1827 began in a melancholy fashion with the illness and death of Beethoven, it also marked the beginning of Schubert's work on one of his most famous compositions, the song cycle *Die Winterreise*, or "Winter Journey."

Summer's heat brought stinking air to the dirty and polluted city, but Franz was again lucky enough to be able to leave. He traveled to the homes of his admirers, including members of the Styrian Music Society in Graz. They all loved his work.

After such a pleasant summer holiday, Franz's return to Vienna was accompanied by more illness and depression. "I am finding it very hard to settle down in Vienna again," he complained in a letter. "It is big enough, to be sure, but on the other hand it is devoid of open-heartedness and sincerity, of genuine ideas and sensible talk and above all, of intellectual accomplishments."

Despite Vienna's drawbacks, he managed to finish *Die Winterreise*. His friends, who had disliked it at first, soon realized that it too was a masterpiece.

Franz also continued to enjoy the city's bars and coffeehouses. In January of 1828, one of the biggest-ever Schubertiads took place. The occasion was the celebration of his friend Spaun's engagement. For lifelong bachelor Franz Schubert, the event must have held a touch of sadness. His melancholy would have only increased if he'd known it would be the last Schubertiad he'd enjoy.

Two months later, he bowed to pressure from his friends and organized a concert of his own music. It was a financial success, and the audience also enjoyed it. "Everybody was lost in a frenzy of admiration and rapture," wrote one admirer. Short reviews in newspapers in Berlin, Dresden and Leipzig mentioned it favorably.

But the Viennese press completely ignored it. With the bad luck that dogged Schubert for so much of his life, the famous Italian virtuoso violinist Nicolo Paganini performed three days later. Paganini got all the attention.

And soon afterward, Schubert sent his Ninth Symphony to the Society of Music Lovers in Vienna. But they rejected it. It was too hard to play, the orchestra members said. It would remain unperformed for more than a decade. Also known as the "Great C Major" Symphony, it compares favorably with anything that Beethoven ever wrote.

Even as his illness progressed into its final stages, publishers continued to hound Franz for new songs. He continued to write, but in September he was so weak that he moved into his brother Ferdinand's house. The next month, perhaps imagining his own burial, he traveled 50 miles to visit the grave site of Joseph Haydn, a composer who had influenced both Mozart and Beethoven. And his creative output continued. He wrote six new works that month. During his last weeks, Spaun and many other friends were regular visitors.

Then in mid-November, he was confined to his bed. "I am ill," he wrote to Schober, as though his friend needed reminding. "I have had nothing to eat or drink for eleven days now, and can only wander feebly and uncertainly between armchair and bed. So, please be so good as to come to my aid in this desperate condition with something to read." Schober sent him a book. But perhaps unaware of how serious and life-threatening this illness was, he neglected to visit.

A few days after writing the letter, Schubert became delirious. Then in mid-afternoon on November 19, 1828, Franz Schubert looked up into his brother's face and said, "Here. Here is my end." With that, he died.

Franz Schubert, a man who'd known so much pain in his lifetime, was finally at peace. He was not yet 32 years old. Even Mozart, the symbol of the great composer snatched away prematurely by death, lived more than four years longer than Schubert.

Spaun wrote, "Poor Schubert, so young and at the start of such a brilliant career. What a wealth of untapped treasures his death has robbed us of!"

The composer passed away owing money, so his friends took up a collection to pay for a proper burial. By 1830, they'd raised enough money to erect a monument at his gravesite in the Wahring Cemetery, not far from where Beethoven was also buried. Grillparzer, the orator at Beethoven's funeral, wrote a poem in Schubert's honor. Part of it appears on the monument: "Here lies buried a rich treasure, and yet more glorious hopes."

"No one understands another's grief, no one understands another's joy," Schubert once explained. "My music is the product of my talent and my misery. And that which I have written in my greatest distress is what the world seems to like best."

Although the world scarcely acknowledged the composer during his brief lifetime, it has never stopped celebrating his work since his death. ◆

FYI

COFFEE
PEOPLE

Whether we're impatiently waiting for our morning latte or meeting friends for an afternoon mocha, we love our coffee shops. Nearly two centuries ago in Vienna, Franz Schubert felt the same way.

He was living in the right place, because Vienna was where the European fondness for coffee began. According to one story, an army of invading Ottoman Turks besieged the city for several months in 1683 before being routed in a battle. The panicked troops left behind several bags of coffee beans. Coffee drinking had long been popular in the Ottoman Empire but was unknown in Europe.

A man who had served as a spy behind the Turkish lines knew about coffee. He brewed up some of the "Turkish drink" for doubtful Viennese. A few sips quickly removed their doubts.

Within a few years, coffee houses had sprung up all over Vienna. When customers entered, they would seat themselves. Then a waiter would approach to take their order. There were about two dozen types of coffee drinks to choose from, including mochas! When the order was ready, it was brought over with a cold glass of water and a newspaper. The waiter would occasionally return to freshen the water or offer a new paper, but unlike the hurried atmosphere in modern chain coffee shops, the establishments of Schubert's day were relaxed. A customer could linger until closing time.

Schubert enjoyed this leisurely approach. He would often wake up in mid-morning, spend a few hours working on his compositions and then stroll to a nearby coffee shop. Sometimes, he would get a musical idea and jot it on a scrap of napkin or an old menu, other days he'd meet friends, hanging out until the day's end.

Part of the reason for the pleasant, unrushed atmosphere of Viennese coffee shops was the city they operated in. "The whole aspect of the town with its surroundings, has something about it suggestive of riches, well-being and personal contentment," explained writer Varnhagen von Ense. "The people here seem healthier and happier than elsewhere."

Maybe it was the coffee. Today many of the cafes frequented by Franz Schubert and his friends remain—such as the Café Bogner and the Café Hugelmann—barely changed by progress, just waiting for someone with time to kill and a need for caffeine.

Selected Works

Note: Numbers are based on the Thematic Catalogue of Schubert's Works by Otto Erich Deutsch. This book provides the generally-accepted method of cataloging Schubert's works.

D 1	Fantasia in G for Piano Duet
D 4	Overture to "Der Teufel als Hydraulicus"
D 5	Song "Hagar's Klage"
D 6	Song "Des Mädchens Klage"
D 18	String Quartet #1 (in mixed keys)
D 32	String Quartet #2 in C
D 33	Settings of "Entra l'uomo allor che nasce" for various voices
D 48	Fantasia in C for Piano Duet called "Grande Sonate"
D 50	Song "Die Schatten"
D 157	Sonata (#1) in E for Piano
D 167	Mass #2 in G major
D 328	Song "Erlkönig"
D 385	Sonatina in A for Piano and Violin op. posth. 137 #2
D 485	Symphony #5 in B flat
D 550	Song "Die Forelle"
D 644	Rosamunde Overture in C minor
D 664	Sonata #13 in A major, opus 120
D 667	Quintet for Piano and strings in A major, "Forellen"
D 668	Overture in G for piano duet
D 759	Symphony #8 in B called "Unfinished" two complete movements and nine bars of a Scherzo
D 760	Fantasia in C, "Wanderer Fantasy,"opus 15
D 780	Six Moments Musicaux for piano, opus 94
D 795	Song Cycle "Die Schöne Müllerin," opus 25
D 803	Octet in F for string and wind instruments op. posth. 166
D 804	String Quartet #13 in A, opus 29
D 810	String Quartet #14 in D Minor, "Death and the Maiden"
D 850	Sonata #17 in D, opus 53
D 899	Impromptu for piano in G flat major, No. 3
D 911	Song Cycle "Die Winterreise"
D 929	Piano Trio in E flat
D 935	Impromptu No. 2 in A flat major
D 940	Fantasia for Four Hands in F minor
D 944	Symphony #9 in C
D 950	Mass #6 in E flat for Quartet, mixed chorus, and orchestra
D 957	Song Cycle "Schwanengesang"
D 958	Sonata #19 in C for piano
D 959	Sonata #20 in A for piano
D 960	Sonata #21 in B flat for piano

Chronology

1797   born in Vienna on January 31

1808   joins Imperial Boys Choir and accepted to Stadtkonvikt boarding school

1812   mother dies; begins studying composition with Antonio Salieri

1813   leaves Stadtkonvikt; composes First Symphony

1814   trains as public school teacher; falls in love with Therese Grob

1816   quits teaching job to focus full time on writing music and moves in with Franz von Schober

1817   returns home

1818   takes summer job as music teacher for children of Count Esterházy

1821   first "Schubertiad" is held

1823   realizes that he has contracted syphilis

1824   makes second visit to summer home of Count Esterházy

1825   discovers his growing fame during tour of Austria

1827   serves as torchbearer at funeral for Ludwig van Beethoven

1828   dies in Vienna on November 19

Historical footnote: Franz Schubert's official cause of death was listed as "nervous fever." Many experts since the time of his death in 1828 have determined his cause of death to be syphilis and typhus. It was common practice in nineteenth century Europe for the family to put up a smokescreen in dealing with sexually transmitted diseases. As is the case today, these diseases carried a stigma. For this reason, you might read conflicting information about Schubert's early demise. All evidence available today points to the ultimate cause of death as typhoid fever in a man already afflicted with syphilis.

1789   fall of the Bastille in Paris begins French Revolution

1791   Wolfgang Amadeus Mozart dies

1793   French King Louis XVI and Queen Marie Antoinette beheaded

1797   Napoleon Bonaparte's first war with Austria

1799   George Washington dies

1801   Robert Fulton invents first submarine

1803   Meriwether Lewis and William Clark begin exploration of Western United States

1804   Napoleon declared Emperor of France

1809   composer Joseph Haydn dies

1812   Great Britain and the U.S. begin War of 1812

1814   British invade Washington, D.C.

1815   British and US troops fight Battle of New Orleans, not knowing that peace treaty ending War of 1812 had been signed several weeks earlier

1817   construction of Erie Canal begins and lasts eight years; it connects Great Lakes and Atlantic Ocean via Hudson River

1818   Canada and U.S. agree that 49th parallel will be border between the two countries

1820   U.S. Congress approves Missouri Compromise—Maine is admitted to the Union as a free state, Missouri admitted as slave state

1823   "A Visit from Saint Nicholas" by Clement Moore is first published in *Troy Sentinel*

1824   first performance of Beethoven's Ninth ("Choral") Symphony

1826   Thomas Jefferson and John Adams, two of most famous signers of Declaration of Independence, both die on July 4th, the 50th anniversary of the signing

1828   Russian novelist Leo Tolstoy is born

1837   Queen Victoria of England begins 64-year reign

For Further Reading

Books For Young Adults

Thompson, Wendy. *Composer's World: Franz Schubert*. New York: Viking Press, 1991.

Time-Life Books Editors. *What Life Was Like in Europe's Romantic Era*. Alexandria, VA: Time-Life Books, 2000.

Ventura, Piero. *Great Composers*. New York: G.P. Putnam's Sons, 1988.

Young, Percy M. *Masters of Music: Schubert*. New York: David White, 1970.

On the Web

Biography, List of Works, Photos
http://w3.rz-berlin.mpg.de/cmp/schubert.html

Franz Peter Schubert: Master of Song
http://classicalmus.hispeed.com/articles/schubert.html

Musical Listing
http://www.classical.net/music/comp.lst/schubert.html

Works Consulted

Brown, Maurice John Edwin. *The New Grove Schubert*. New York: W.W. Norton, 1997.

Brown, Maurice John Edwin. *Schubert: A Critical Biography*. Cambridge, MA: DeCapo Press, 1977.

Cooper, Barry. *Beethoven*. New York: Oxford University Press, 2000.

Deutsch, Otto Erich (editor). *Franz Schubert's Letters and Other Writings*. Westport, CT: Greenwood Press, 1970.

Erickson, Raymond, ed., *Schubert's Vienna*. New Haven, CT: Yale University Press, 1997

Friedenthal, Richard. *Goethe: His Life and Times*. New York: World Publishing Company, 1963.

Gibbs, Christopher H., ed. *The Cambridge Companion to Schubert*. New York: Cambridge University Press, 1997.

McCay, Elizabeth Norman. *Franz Schubert: A Biography*. Oxford: Clarendon Press, 1996.

McLynn, Frank. *Napoleon: A Biography*. New York: Arcade Publishing, 2002.

Newbould, Brian. *Schubert: The Music and the Man*. Berkeley, CA: University of California Press, 1997.

Osborne, Charles. *Schubert and His Vienna*. New York: Alfred A. Knopf, 1985.

Reed, John. *Schubert*. New York: Oxford University Press, 2001.

Wechsberg, Joseph. *Schubert: His Life, His Work, His Time*. New York: Rizzoli, 1977.

Woodford, Peggy. *Schubert*. New York: Omnibus, 1987.

Glossary

aria (ah-REE-uh) - solo song in an opera

composer (kum-POHZ-er) - someone who creates a work of music

concerto (kon-CHERT-oh) - an orchestral piece featuring an instrumental solo

counterpoint - blending of two or more melodies

opera (AHP-rah) - a dramatic piece where the lines are sung rather than spoken

patron (PAY-tron) - someone who supports an artist, usually financially

prostitute (pros-TIH-toot)- woman who gives sexual favors for money

song cycle - group of songs linked by both lyrics and music

sonata (suh-NOT-ah) - a work written for one or two instruments

soprano (sup-RAN-oh) - a singing voice which is in the highest range

symphony (SIM-foh-nee) - a large-scale orchestral work, usually written in four movements

virtuoso (vert-chew-OH-soh) - an extremely skilled musical instrument player

Index